Trixie

* * * and * * *

the Razzle-Dazzle Ruse

Written by G. M. Berrow

(L)(B)

Little, Brown and Company
New York Boston

Little, Brown and Company
Hachette Book Group
1290 Avenue of the Americas, New York, NY 10104
Visit us at lb-kids.com
mylittlepony.com

First Edition: March 2017

Little, Brown and Company is a division of Hachette Book Group, Inc. The Little, Brown name and logo are trademarks of Hachette Book Group, Inc.

The publisher is not responsible for websites (or their content) that are not owned by the publisher.

Library of Congress Control Number 2016954136

ISBNs: 978-0-316-30163-3 (paperback); 978-0-316-30164-0 (ebook)

Printed in the United States of America

LSC-C

10 9 8 7 6 5 4 3 2

For Josh Dean,
John Feulner, and the
Baltimore convention
that celebrates the
Magic of friendship and
community

CONTENTS

* * *

CHAPTER 13

Chapter

1

A grand Entrance

✶✶✶

The blue Unicorn leaned back, tilting her chin high to the sky to catch a glimpse of the tip-top of the highest castle spire. Her long, pointy wizard's hat fell backward off her head and tumbled to the shimmering floor. "Oh fizz!" she grunted, fumbling to pick it up. She squashed the wide purple brim down over her pale-blue mane again.

"Helloooooo?" Trixie knocked her hoof again, growing impatient. It took all her willpower to refrain from using a glittering smoke bomb to vanish and reappear inside. She was following the rules. Twilight Sparkle loved rules. So first she would knock. Then Trixie would be welcomed into the Castle of Friendship for an extended stay.

Nopony knew she was coming. She usually parked her wagon near the castle and camped out. But this time, Trixie thought it might be nice to stay in the comforts of a place that had more room to stretch her hooves. It was a gigantic castle, for Celestia's sake!

In truth, Trixie had not always gotten along with Twilight. After all that had transpired between the dueling magicians, the two still saw each other as somepony to impress and simultaneously challenge. Even *if* one of the ponies was a "princess" now. Trixie still couldn't fathom that Twilight had received the honor when the two of them really were quite equal in talent and charisma.

But finally, Trixie and Twilight Sparkle had something undeniably special in common: their friendships with Starlight Glimmer. Trixie would never admit it out loud, but it felt wonderful to put the rivalry to rest. Besides, Trixie reasoned, there was still plenty of time for Princess Celestia to decree that Trixie was a princess, too. Stranger things had happened in Equestria before: Princess Luna had once been banished to the moon, Discord had become friends with ponykind, and an entire horde of changelings had been taught to love one another.

It could happen.

Trixie had just begun conjuring images of herself at her grand coronation when the heavy door swung open. A familiar magical aura danced around its edges. Trixie perked up. She'd know that glow anywhere! It was exactly the pony she wanted to see— her new best friend and unexpected confidante, Starlight Glimmer. Trixie exhaled with relief at the friendly face.

"Trixie!" Starlight beamed. "I didn't know you were going to be in Ponyville!" She lifted her hoof and gestured to the cavernous abode. "Come inside and have a slice of apple pie. It's been ages since you've visited me." Starlight was unusually sunny today, for somepony so sarcastic and rebellious. "We have tons to catch up on since that whole epic changeling-hive journey where we saved everypony from certain doom," Starlight joked. "Let's keep it a little more casual this time, eh?"

"The Observant and Suspicious Trixie notices that you are in a particularly great mood." Trixie narrowed her eyes. "Why?"

Starlight smirked. "Can I vent for a minute?" Her face morphed into a frown.

"What are friends for?" Trixie replied, eager to hear the dirt. *This* was the Starlight she knew.

"Well, it's just"—Starlight entered the castle kitchen—"friendship lessons are great and all, but sometimes I feel I'm not getting anywhere." She sighed. "I guess that's it. It's just a little frustrating."

That was the big venting session? "Oh," said Trixie, trying to hide her disappointment. It's not that she wanted things between Starlight and Twilight to be unpleasant; Trixie just wanted Starlight to like her best. Was that so much to ask? "Sounds rough!"

The purple Unicorn activated her magic to open the pastry cupboard, where an enticingly fragrant apple pie with a latticed crust sat. "At least I finally know how to bake the perfect pie, thanks to Applejack. Can you believe that we baked this using zero magic, just the Apple family recipe and good old-fashioned hoof grease? Here—have some." Starlight's smile beamed with pride.

The golden crust shone as Starlight put the pie in front of her guest. Trixie took a huge bite and spoke through it. "I don't understand—you're actually happy to be doing slow, boring things with Twilight and baking pies?" A confetti of flaky crumbs rained down.

"Well, yeah." Starlight shook her purple-and-teal mane. "But I'm also happy because the second you showed up, I realized I have been working *way* too hard lately," she explained. "I need to have some totally wacky, pointless fun, and you're the perfect pony to join me! What do ya say?" Starlight smiled hopefully.

"Pointless fun?" Trixie raised a judgmental brow. "What's the point of that?" She hoped this project wasn't going to hinder her best friend's ability to help her with her very important magical mission.

"To enjoy ourselves! There doesn't have to be a reason." Starlight laughed and added, "Pinkie Pie taught me that."

Trixie grunted in response.

"Gosh, Trixie. When did you become such a hoof-in-the-mud?"

"All right, sheesh. We will go find some *frivolity*." Trixie rolled her eyes. "But can we do it after you help me on *my* project?"

"Sure!" Starlight Glimmer took a bite and gave Trixie a sideways glance. "What is this mysterious project that can't wait?"

"Well, that's the problem," Trixie admitted impatiently. "I don't *know* yet. But I do know I have to come up with a brilliant new act practically by *yesterday*!"

Starlight ate the last bite of her pie and licked the leftover crumbs from her hoof. "Well, sitting around here isn't going to inspire us." She looked around the cavernous, echoing room. Twilight and Spike weren't even home at the moment. Starlight sprang up and slammed her hooves on the table. "Come on, Trixie! We're going for a trot around Ponyville."

"Ponyville is *supposed* to be the friendliest town in Equestria and all that." The slight hint of hometown pride in Starlight Glimmer's voice rubbed Trixie the wrong way. She was start-ing to sound just like Twilight! Ponyville was okay and all, a great place to pass through and do a performance or two, but Trixie had never really seen the fuss. Starlight nudged her. "Maybe if you try saying hello to some ponies, you'll relax a bit...."

"Relax?" Trixie's smile morphed into a yawn. "Brilliant idea! Maybe Princess Luna will give me an idea for my new magic act in my dreams." Small talk with random ponies was a complete waste of time. Trixie turned on her hoof and started back toward the castle. *"Byeee!"*

"Hey, wait!" Starlight exclaimed, shooting some magic at Trixie. A glittery orb surrounded her, rendering her unable to walk any farther. Trixie pouted and knocked her hoof against the force field. Her eyes darted back and forth as she checked for wayward onlookers. The last thing Trixie needed was a bunch of ponies seeing that she, the Great and Powerful Trixie, couldn't even escape from a simple shield spell! It would tarnish her reputation as a magician. "Let me out of here this instant!"

"Oops!" Starlight said. "Sorry." Sometimes she was a bit too impulsive with her spells. She sent a counter zap at the bubble, which popped immediately. Trixie tumbled to the ground, looking quite grumpy.

Trixie feigned a yawn. "Bor-ing." Trixie stood up and brushed herself off with the corner of her starry purple cloak. "Enough of this meandering! I've got a much better way to spend our time, O Wise and Brilliant assistant Starlight!"

Starlight frowned. "But I—"

"Hush, best friend!" Trixie interrupted. "Trixie has something of greater importance to achieve. You see, this brand-new magic act that we're going to create has to be the best I've ever performed because..." Trixie trailed off as a wave of nerves rushed through her. Her knees felt wobbly. "Because..."

Starlight Glimmer raised her brow, waiting. "...Because?"

"Because I'm about to be the first magician accepted into the Starmane Society of Magicians since the Lunar Return!" Trixie was practically bubbling over with anticipation. "How, you may ask, am I going to achieve this impossible task? The answer is obvious. I am going to attempt a brand-new feat of magical trickery, the bravest stunt to have ever been dreamed up by anypony throughout the history of magicians. And you're going to help me. Now, where's my room? I'm going to need *a lot* of practice space."

"Your room?" Starlight had barely said anything before Trixie took off back toward the castle in a gallop. "Wait up!" Starlight shouted as she ran after the rogue magician. "Let me help you choose one!" Starlight recalled the secret, magical suite she'd recently discovered in the castle. It had turned out to be an Andalusian Amplifier, causing any magic performed inside to go haywire and create a vortex! There was no telling what might happen if Trixie found one of those. "Trixie, wait!" Starlight called out.

As Trixie burst through the front doors of the castle and ran through the halls, the blue Unicorn couldn't help but chuckle to herself. What harm was there in a little impromptu disappearing trick? She loved to keep her audience guessing, and her best friend, Starlight, was no exception. It was all part of the show.

Chapter

2

Sleight of Hoof

★ ★ ★

Even though she still had to come up with the perfect magical act, Trixie got right to work on the rest of her impressively extensive to-do list around Ponyville the next day. *No time to waste when Trixie is preparing to achieve the impossible!* she thought to herself as she whipped up a hearty breakfast of toast, juice, and cinnamon-sugar oatmeal for her hosts. True, it was an attempt to ingratiate herself to Twilight and Starlight. But it seemed to be working. The ponies devoured the delicious meal and seemed quite surprised at her brilliant cooking skills. "Wow, Trixie," Twilight Sparkle marveled through a mouth full of cinnamon-sugar. "This oatmeal is delectable! What spell did you use to make it?"

"No spell. Just another thing that I'm amazing at!" she sang, only to be met with a double eye roll. After the three ponies ate, Trixie shooed her reluctant hosts away. She promised to clean up and give them some quiet time to work on their "important friendship lessons." Trixie wasn't positive, but she thought Twilight kept looking over her shoulder at Trixie as she left the room. She looked impressed!

Once the two of them were busy, Trixie slipped away and marched right to the Carousel Boutique, ignoring their warnings not to bother Rarity. Apparently, the Unicorn was immersed in a project of her own, sewing a dress for some fashion event. *Pish*, thought Trixie as she trotted through Ponyville. *Fashion, smashion.*

"I love fashion!" Trixie shouted as she burst through the front door. She took a seat on one of the velvet loungers and made herself quite comfortable. "The Great and Powerful Trixie has graced you with her presence because she would like to commission a cloak of utmost importance...." Trixie stood up decidedly.

"*Today*." She stuck her nose in the air and closed her eyes as if to illustrate the seriousness of her demand.

"Oh, Trixie, you do know how to make an entrance, darling." Rarity laughed, putting a polished gray hoof to her chest. "Which I, of all ponies, can appreciate." She continued pushing a pearly swathe of chiffon through the needle of her sewing machine.

"But honestly, darling, I'm afraid I can't do that today. I'm terribly busy with this dress for the Glammy Awards. You know— the glitziest night of the year for anypony who's anypony in fashion, music, or the arts? I cannot let my dear client Sapphire Shores step a single hoof onto the red carpet looking like anything less than pure perfection." Rarity adjusted her red work glasses and looked up at Trixie sympathetically. "So, there will be no cloaks today."

Trixie's face quickly contorted into a mushy frown.

"You can add your name to my commissions list!" Rarity chirped. She waved her hoof to the long list on the wall with a flourish. "But it may take a few moons."

"B-b-but...I *need* a new cloak now!" Trixie whined pathetically. "It's my only chance of *getting in*...." Her lip jutted out. "Please?"

"'Getting in?'" Rarity raised a brow. Now her interest was piqued. "To something exclusive?" She stood up and trotted over to a ponnequin wearing a gauzy white gown. As she fluffed the voluminous petticoats, the fabric seemed to dance and swirl in the light. Trixie couldn't take her eyes off it.

"The Starmane Society of Magicians!" Trixie exclaimed, stomping her hoof on the floor for emphasis. "Also known as the only organization of magicians that means any-thing, anywhere. I simply *must* be made an offer of membership or I might as well not be a magician at all!"

The swish of the fabric was silenced as Rarity paused. "At all?" She was intrigued. Ha! Nopony could resist Trixie's charms.

"Well"—Trixie smiled—"it's practically impossible to audition for Starmane, but my plan is more solid than a rock farm's foun-dation." The pony began to pace around the room, gesticulating wildly with her hoof as she spoke. "First step: Have the most magnificent fashion designer in Equestria design me a new look. That's where you come in, Rarity!

"Then, while you're busy working *your* magic, I'm going to stay here in Ponyville practicing *my* jaw-dropping feat of magical genius in front of a live pony audience until it's flawless. Finally, I will sneak into the Grand Magician's Ball and perform it for the entire committee of Starmane elders. They won't be able to tear their eyes away from my incredible talents, and then they'll have to make me a member right on the spot. Ha!" Trixie was wild-eyed.

"You've been invited to a grand ball?" Rarity cooed, clearly missing the entire point of Trixie's speech. Trixie could practically see Rarity's mind racing with visions of taffeta and couture headdresses. Rarity batted her eyelashes. "Do you get a plus one? For your designer?"

"Uh…" Trixie laughed nervously and took a seat back on the velvet sofa. She pawed at a turquoise cushion. "I haven't actually been *invited*, but—"

"Oh, Trixie." Rarity shook her purple mane. "Attending a gala you've not been invited to is rather passé, no?"

"Not when it's the only way for a pony to get noticed," Trixie replied. She expelled a puff of air and slumped down. She was really trying to ham it up.

"I truly wish I could help you, but this Glammys dress really needs my attention." Rarity trotted back over to her creation draped on the ponnequin and started sending little zaps of magic from her horn to the fabric.

Each time the magic touched a button or a seam, there was a tiny sizzle that activated a subtle glow. Rarity was admiring her work in the three-way mirror when she caught a glimpse of Trixie's sad face.

"On the other hoof"—Rarity spun around—"I might have a little extra time to fit it in. *After* the dress is finished."

"Excellent!" Trixie beamed, trotting over to join her at the ponnequin. "Make it just like this." Trixie gestured to the gown. The mesmerizing garment glittered as it rotated. "You could just lose a layer of these excessive petticoats and sew it into a cloak for me right now!"

Rarity frowned and kept on working. "That's not what I agreed to—and I really don't have time right now. I still have to add some gold trim here and there—"

"Here, I'll show you!" interrupted Trixie as she dove for the fabric. At the very same moment, Rarity sent a zap of glowing gold magic to the hem. It hit Trixie's right forehoof with a sizzle.

"Ouchies!" Trixie winced, losing her balance. As if in slow motion, the blue Unicorn tripped over her other hooves, knocking into a side table. A glass of water teetered precariously. Trixie reached her hoof out to try to stop the glass. *"Nooo!"* Another zap of magic shot from Trixie's horn right at the dress as the water splashed down. As the holding spell took effect, the drenched skirts began to tear apart. Rarity quickly shot a zap of her own glowing magic at the dress to counteract it, but it was too late. The dress was torn and wet.

"My beautiful work!" Rarity cried out in horror. She shook her purple mane in disbelief.

"Whoopsies?" replied Trixie, massaging her hoof, which now pulsed with soreness. Rarity didn't have to say anything in response—the annoyed grimace on her face said it all. Trixie backed out of the shop with a humble shrug and a wink.

So far, the unstoppable magic show was looking more like a pitiful dress rehearsal—where the dress was ruined. And there was no new cloak.

Chapter

3

Tricks of the Trade

✦ ✦ ✦

"Come on!" Trixie called out to her reluctant assistant. She looked over her shoulder, brimming with enthusiasm. Trixie couldn't wait to get started setting everything up for the magic show tonight. So what if there'd been a silly accident? The greatest and most powerful Unicorn in all of Equestria wasn't going to let a tiny little thing like a torn dress derail her. Even if it was for a "pop star." *Sapphire Shores, Sapphire schmores.*

It's not like anypony had been hurt, other than Trixie herself. One little sore hoof was no big deal. Rarity would come around again to the idea of sewing her a new cloak eventually. The most important aspect wasn't the costume anyway—it was the daring magic.

All Trixie needed was her best friend on board to help out. "Hurry up, Starlight!"

"Are you sure about this?" Starlight trotted two paces behind Trixie. It was as if she wanted to give her friend enough space to change her mind. Not that she would.

Once Trixie set her mind to something, she would not let the matter drop. "I'm positive," she declared. "The only way for me to perfect the trick I intend to do in front of the Starmane Society elders is to practice it in front of a live audience." Her eyes lit up as they rounded the corner and her traveling wagon of tricks came into sight. "And you're going to be my assistant, right?"

"Of course." Starlight nodded. She clearly still felt guilty about the last time Trixie had tried to put on a show in Ponyville. Starlight had agreed to help Trixie with her feat, "The Moonshot Manticore Mouthdive." In the stunt (originated by the great Hoofdini), Trixie was all set to launch herself from a cannon into the mouth of a hungry manticore before reappearing unharmed inside a magic box.

But Twilight's dinner party with Princess Celestia had gotten in the way of things, and Starlight Glimmer had almost let down one of the only ponies she was truly able to call her friend. Trixie had forgiven Starlight, but the memory still stung a little.

"So, what did you decide on for your grand trick?" she asked as she followed Trixie up the steps of her wagon and inside her traveling abode. The place was littered with scrolls of parchment, costume pieces, and empty applesauce packets.

"It's 'The Tears of the Dragon'!" She spun around, her cloak knocking a purple top hat onto the floor. A confused bunny hopped out.

Trixie's violet eyes sparkled deviously. "The Clever and Inventive Trixie came up with it herself this morning after breakfast. It is sure to deliver the equal amounts of shock and awe necessary to catch the discerning eyes of the highest-ranking Star-mane Society ponies!" She changed her tone to a more matter-of-fact one. "Besides, each applicant won't even be considered for membership unless he or she comes up with a brand-new, never-before-attempted daring feat of magical trickery."

"See? I told you that taking a walk around Ponyville would inspire you!" Starlight replied. She brushed some colored scarves off the sofa and took a seat. "So, how does it work?"

Trixie unfurled a giant scroll with a complex series of drawings on it. Starlight followed the progression of the images in disbelief. The last frame was filled with arrows and feathers, surrounded by hundreds of fiery raindrops. A massive, angry dragon sat in the center. The scribbled likeness of Trixie stood on top of him, hooves held out in triumph.

"Whoa!" Starlight Glimmer pulled a face. "Am I reading this correctly?" She pointed her hoof at the fire-breathing dragon. "You're going to tickle a dragon with a feather so much that it cries dragon funny tears—the hottest-known substance to ponykind—then perform a dance routine while they rain down on you, culminating in your disappearance into thin air before you will then reappear on top of the dragon to put the very feather you tickled it with in your performance hat?!" Starlight's eyes were as large as saucers.

"Precisely." Trixie smirked. "Good thing Trixie knows what she's doing."

She began to trot around, gathering various items into a saddlebag. "Oh good—my dragon whistle!" She picked up the prop, shined it on her starry cloak, and tossed it in. "Now, where did I put those feathers?" Trixie rifled around in her mess but had little luck. Finally, she picked up a pillow and tore it open. It exploded, and feathers rained down on every surface.

"You don't have to do this, you know..." Starlight put her hoof on Trixie's shoulder. "I wouldn't want anything to happen to you."

Trixie spit out a mouthful of feathers and laughed. "I'm touched by your concern, but give me a *break*, Starlight. I'm great and powerful! Everything is going to go exactly as I want it to."

Chapter

4

A Razzle-Dazzle Rehearsal

★ ★ ★

The new-and-improved traveling stage setup, which had been recently built for "The Humble and Penitent Trixie's Great Equestrian Apology Tour," was officially back in Ponyville. It was quite grand—a true step up from the rinky-dink stage Trixie used to drag from town to town.

Two large posters depicting a dramatic Trixie inside a ring of fire hung on either side of the wooden platform. Shimmery curtains held up by cardboard stars were draped above. A spotlight illuminated the center of the stage, and exciting music blasted from the speakers. It was more than enough to draw attention. Sure enough, it wasn't long before curious ponies began to gather and wait in anticipation of the show.

Backstage, Starlight Glimmer stole a peek through the shiny blue curtains at the growing crowd. She hoped Trixie was right about the safety of her daring display.

Whatever happened, Starlight would do her best to diffuse the situation and protect everypony—even if that meant shooting wayward force fields everywhere to do so.

"How do I look?" Trixie asked, striking a pose in her old purple starry hat and cloak. She smiled devilishly. "Don't tell me, I already know."

"You look great!" Starlight lied, forcing an encouraging smile. *Powerful!* In truth, the costume now appeared lackluster in comparison to the extravagant stage. Perhaps Trixie had been right earlier about needing a new cloak.

"That means the Great and Powerful Trixie is ready to attempt 'The Tears of the Dragon'!" Trixie tossed the silver whistle to Starlight Glimmer. "You remember your cue?"

Starlight nodded. "When you say 'Behold the fearsome dragon,' I blow the whistle." Starlight pointed her hoof at a hose. "And then I turn that on after you tickle the beast?"

"Yes!" Trixie's eyes were alight with a fiery determination. It was not unlike the one that had possessed her when she wore the cursed Alicorn Amulet and tried to control all of Ponyville. Trixie giggled with glee. "It's going to be so dangerous and impressive." Starlight shot her an admonishing look. *"Whaaat?"* Trixie replied innocently. "That's the name of the game."

Without further ado, Trixie trotted over to the side and pulled a lever. The curtains swung apart, and the blue Unicorn stepped out onto the stage.

The audience stomped their hooves on the ground in applause. They'd been waiting a long time, which always amped up the anticipation to an appropriate level.

"Welcome, mares and gentlecolts, to the greatest show, the most memorable feat you

will ever lay eyes upon!" Trixie did a the-
atrical twirl. Her pale-blue mane and tail
whipped out in time with her cloak. "The
Great and Powerful Trixie's one-of-a-kind
stunt—'The Tears of the *Draaaaagon*'!

"I have yet to even test out this daring
feat." The crowd gasped. Trixie smiled glee-
fully and continued on. "So if you are faint
of heart—avert your eyes! If you care to wit-
ness the glory of my magical prowess, do
not dare to tear them away.

"Behold the fearsome dragon!" Trixie said
through her gritted-teeth smile. Starlight
trotted onstage, eyes darting around. She
blew the whistle. At once, the entire crowd
felt the fiery heat of the gigantic beast.

Trixie tried to raise her hooves way up
high to gesture toward the approaching
dragon, but suddenly her right forehoof

seemed extra heavy. She struggled with its weight, barely lifting it the height of her shoulder. The crowd gasped.

Trixie's hoof was pulsating with an eerie golden glow.

Chapter

5

The Big Reveal
★ ★ ★

"Ahhhhh!" Trixie screamed as she held up her hoof to inspect it. Not only was it glowing, it was now completely transparent!

Starlight galloped over. "What's happening, Trixie? You didn't tell me about this part!" she whispered in a panic. "Is this part of the act?"

"N-n-n-*nooo!*" Trixie shook her head in disbelief. Was this really happening to her while she was onstage, mid-trick? It was like an embarrassing dream, except it was real. She looked out to the audience. Ponies shielded their eyes as the hoof grew brighter. "Help me, Starlight!" she whispered out of the side of her mouth.

"I have an idea!" Starlight snapped into action. She galloped across the stage with a showy flourish as she retrieved the hose. Starlight used her magic to turn on the flow of water and tilt it up at an angle to create a beautiful, misty spray.

It obscured the stage with the combination of water and light from Trixie's pulsing hoof, creating a dewy rainbow-filled curtain. It was enough to distract the crowd temporarily.

Starlight Glimmer was trying to think of what to do next when a gigantic red dragon landed on the stage! It screeched as it dove low above the heads of the ponies in the crowd. They looked up in surprise as the dragon's massive wings caused gusts of air to blow through their manes. The dragon dove straight through the mist and burst through the back of the stage before taking off into the sky.

The crowd *oooh*ed and *aaah*ed. It didn't even matter that the part of the trick where the dragon was going to cry funny tears hadn't happened.

It was music to Trixie's ears. She forgot all about her afflicted hoof and stepped out into the water to receive the praise and take a bow. Water rained down on her as she did her signature twirl. "Another impressive performance by the Great and Powerful *Trixieeeee*!"

Within seconds, a small spray of golden droplets rained down onto the crowd, solidifying in midair like a sparkling hailstorm. The ponies close enough to the stage pulled them from their manes and retrieved them from the ground. Their faces glowed as they held the stone pieces in their hooves in awe.

"What is it?" asked one.

"It's beautiful!" cried another.

"It's Glowpaz!" shouted a pale-pink Pegasus. She held up a large piece in victory.

The aqua-colored Earth pony next to her smiled. "That's one of the most valuable gems in Equestria!" The rest of the ponies scrambled to find a Glowpaz drop.

"*Uhhhhhhh...*" Trixie laughed nervously. "*Voilà?*" She glanced across the stage and met Starlight's eye. Her friend's gaze seemed to say, *What exactly just happened here?* Trixie gave her a tiny wink and maintained her hundred-watt smile. Because whatever odd spell Trixie had just conjured, it had been a Big Reveal to even the magician herself.

The sky was darkening over Ponyville as Trixie trudged to her favorite spot on the edge of the Everfree Forest. *"Euuugh!"* Trixie grunted, trying to lift her heavy hoof. Beads of sweat trickled down her muzzle. She was starting to feel a deep sense of dread inside. Despite the fact that Trixie had achieved her goal of impressing everypony, she knew that something was very wrong with her hoof. If she could only make it to her favorite thinking spot, she might be able to make some sense of the night's odd events.

Finally, Trixie saw it. The trees arched in a frame over a secluded grassy spot that brushed a curve in the river. Trixie had stopped there on numerous occasions while passing through Ponyville. It was perfect for freshening up after a long day, which Trixie was desperately in need of right now.

The troublesome interaction with Rarity was still bothering her, but the truth was that Trixie couldn't riddle out was the wonky performance. She replayed in her mind the events of the bizarre show as she dragged her leaden hoof through the dirt.

Trixie plopped down for a moment, exhausted. She held her heavy hoof up to her face for inspection. It was still glowing, but more faintly. Originally, the shock of seeing her hoof glow had thrown off Trixie. But she couldn't deny the way she'd impressed the crowd with the water trick. It was a response she'd never felt from any audience before! Trixie had shocked them. She had *awed* them! It almost didn't matter to her that "The Tears of the Dragon" hadn't gone according to her plan. Maybe this glow-hoof trick was better than her original idea! It would really set her apart from other magicians hoping to woo the Starmane Society.

An image of Starmane herself pinning a Society brooch onto Trixie's cloak danced around in her head. With this new talent, she was unstoppable.

But by the time Trixie had arrived at the water's edge, the glow had pulsed to a faint light. "No, no, no!" Trixie whined as it faded away. She picked up her hoof with ease, the heaviness magically removed and the blue color restored. She was so disappointed that her glowing idea had fizzled out that she didn't even feel like dipping her hooves into the cool stream anymore. She jumped in quickly and then stepped out again, slumping down in defeat. "Guess I'll just head back to the castle," Trixie mumbled to herself. So the pony took off back toward the castle at a gallop, failing to notice the tiny mass of glistening Glowpaz stones now forming in the river like little stars in a darkened sky.

Chapter

6

The Glow Rush

$$\bigstar \quad \bigstar \quad \bigstar$$

Starlight Glimmer had recently gotten into the habit of waking up very early each morning to have a nice trot before she and Twilight would attend to the friendship business of the day. It was a pleasant time to reflect on all that she had learned so far—everything from how to make new friends to being honest about needing alone time away from her studies. The whole incident where she'd accidentally created a vortex in the castle had been a tough but valuable way to learn *that* lesson.

Starlight awoke at sunrise and promptly set out. She weaved her way through town, watching and saying hello as other Ponyville early birds opened up shop and delivered newspapers. Then she headed toward the fields.

On rare occasions, Starlight Glimmer would venture into the Everfree Forest to search for potion ingredients or interesting plants. Today, she was on a mission.

The fresh smell of exotic foliage hit her muzzle the moment she entered the forest thicket. The big treetops gave her abundant cover. As a result, shade shrouded the land except where shafts of light broke through the trees and illuminated the ground below. Starlight stopped and scanned the bushes.

She had been so worried about Trixie after that weird magic show last night that she'd immediately told Twilight about the debacle. Twilight, in turn, had spent hours poring over books in the library to find anything that might give a clue about Trixie. It was not normal to have one's hoof light up like a bulb. If Twilight's book on plants had been correct, there was a certain exotic plant that just might help.

If Starlight ever managed to find one, that was.

Starlight was confident, but she hoped that she would recognize the Gleam Berries as soon as she saw them. She'd never run into any other ponies in the Everfree Forest, so it would be difficult to get a second opinion until she was back at the castle, and if Twilight was right, that hoof glow was going to start getting a lot worse—and a lot more powerful. Maybe it could start to really hurt Trixie as the magic developed.

The sun was rising over the horizon, illuminating Ponyville with a hazy golden glow. Birds began to chirp, and the smell of fresh grass and flowers wafted through the sweet, breezy air. As Starlight came upon a little stream near the edge of the forest, she felt a sense of contentment, even if it was underscored with worry for Trixie. Why did her friend need so much attention that she constantly put herself in harm's way just for the approval of other ponies? A sudden memory interrupted Starlight's musings.

Well, Starlight thought, *Trixie may want attention, but at least she didn't force an entire town of ponies to surrender their cutie marks to her in the name of equality like I did.* Starlight brushed away the memory and blushed crimson even though there was nopony around to hear it or even see her.

"What are you blushin' about there, young filly?" A mare's voice came from the other side of the bushes. Starlight jumped. "Nothin' to be embarrassed about. We high-tailed it straight to this spot when we heard about the sightings, too!"

"Don't startle her, Emerald!" another gruff voice replied. "She looks terrified. You always scare off new friends...."

"That's total hogwash and you know it, Sparky!"

The two voices continued to grumble to each other.

"Uh, hello?" Starlight Glimmer craned her neck, searching for the source. She pushed aside a branch with her hoof and gasped at the sight. An old Unicorn couple had pitched a tent, gathered wood, and whipped up a meal of apple-carrot oatmeal. At least the smells wafting from the bubbling pot perched on the fire implied it.

But aside from all that, it was clearly no ordinary campsite.

The old ponies were hooves-deep in the stream, sifting through pans filled with river rocks. They wore thick magnifying glasses and tall galoshes.

"Told ya she'd come over!" The old stallion turned to Starlight and put out his hoof. "You're welcome to stay for some oatmeal, dearie. But you should know that this is *our* claim we've staked here. So if you're fixin' to get in on this spot, you'd best be movin' on."

"Claim?" Starlight asked in disbelief. "To what?"

"To all the Glowpaz in this section of the forest, of course." He gestured to the river. "We're gonna strike it rich!"

"I got one!" Emerald shouted with unabashed delight. "Lookee here, Sparky!" The mare held up a tiny piece of ore that glinted in the light.

The two ponies held it close to their eyes, which appeared gigantic behind their glasses. Sure enough, it glowed just as Trixie's hoof had at the show!

But how had that piece gotten over here? Starlight was baffled.

"Good luck!" Starlight tried to hide her shock as she replied, backing away through the bushes and circling around their encampment. Though the run-in had been strange, it didn't change the task at hoof—finding some wild Gleam Berries for Trixie.

But as soon as Starlight Glimmer continued trotting down the river, she realized they had a much bigger problem on their hooves. It seemed that Emerald and Sparky weren't the only ones who'd heard about the Glowpaz sightings.

There were dozens of other prospector ponies parking their wagons and getting set up for a long stay in Ponyville! Some of them had even begun to dig holes to search for the gems in the ground, as was evident by the piles of dirt and shovels everywhere.

In an instant, Starlight forgot all about the berries. She took off at a gallop back toward the castle to tell Twilight what she saw and find Trixie. Starlight had to deliver the news.

The fire had been ignited and the glow rush had begun.

Chapter

7

The Hoofi-Cure

★ ★ ★

Trixie peeked inside the front window and knocked gently on the door of the Carousel Boutique. There would be no bursting into rooms and demanding things this time. No—Trixie had to appear humble and penitent. With the razzle-dazzle of her glowing hoof gone, Trixie had to fall back on her old plan of action.

"Anypony there?" Trixie bit her lip and raised her eyebrows hopefully. *"Helloooooo?"*

The door swung open, revealing a haggard-looking Rarity. She'd definitely been working all night. Behind her, Trixie could see that the beautiful ball gown had been repaired successfully. That meant Rarity was finished and would have time to sew her cloak!

"Rarity!" Trixie brightened. "You're looking marvelous today!"

"If you've come to ask about the cloak again"—Rarity shook her mane—"I'm terribly sorry, but—"

"No, no, *no!*" Trixie lied. She looked at the floor and slumped her shoulders for an extra dramatic effect (shoulder slumps always sealed the deal). "I'm here to *apologize* for being such a klutz! As a peace offering, I thought that the two of us might enjoy a nice day at the La Ti Da Spa together." She smiled innocently.

Rarity looked back over her shoulder at the finished dress. She did feel quite exhausted. And keeping Trixie *away* from the dress was probably a good idea…just in case.

"I suppose it would be nice to unwind for just a bit."

Lotus Blossom, a blue spa pony with a pink mane, greeted them at the front desk. "Welcome, Miss Trixie!" she said with a smile. "I have everything you requested all ready to go. Right this way, mares." The fragrance of lavender and cucumber hit their muzzles as they trotted behind Lotus. The pony gestured to two cushy chairs piled with fluffy white towels and robes.

As Rarity settled into her familiar spot, she eyed Trixie. She couldn't help but feel that there was more to Trixie's motives. The pony didn't have a great track record when it came to scheming, but Rarity pushed aside the thought. Everypony deserved another chance.

"So, Trixie," Rarity said, leaning back into her chair. A spa pony named Aloe twisted her mane up into a towel and placed some cucumber slices over her eyelids. She searched her mind for a casual topic of conversation. "What...what have you been up to since you helped rescue everypony from the changeling takeover?"

"That was so crazy, right?!" a familiar high-pitched voice added. A jubilant pink pony bounced over. Pinkie Pie's fuchsia mane was tied up in a towel, but little frizzy pieces of it tried to escape around the edges. She was munching happily on cucumber slices. "What *have* you been up to? Or down to? Or all around to?!"

"Just traveling around Equestria on my tour," Trixie said with an uninterested shrug. This conversation was boring her. She wanted to get to the good stuff—the part where Rarity would agree to make her cloak again. None of this chitter-chatter.

"Oh! I know which one!" Pinkie Pie kept her wide smile. " 'The Humble and Penitent Trixie's Great Equestrian Apology Tour'?"

"That was a *working* title." Trixie sighed in exhaustion and held out her hoof to the spa pony who was preparing to give her a massage and hooficure.

"*Oooh!* What's it called now?!" Pinkie Pie exclaimed between chomps of cucumber slices. " 'The Relaxed and Unperturbed Trixie's La Ti Da Spa Tour'?" Pinkie jumped on her left hooves. "Or 'The Cucumber-Eyed and Bathrobed Trixie's Magical Hoof Tour'?"

Rarity stifled a giggle.

"Neither!" Trixie shot back. "Now, Pinkie Pie, would you kindly leave us alone so we can get to the relaxing part?"

"Okeydokey-lokey!" Pinkie Pie laughed and began to bounce back toward the steam room.

"Wait—what did she say about my hoof?" Trixie lurched forward and the cucumbers slid off her eyes.

Without missing a beat, Pinkie yelled from down the hallway, "It looks all sparkly and weird!"

"It does?" Trixie held her hoof up to her muzzle and noticed that it was glittering with a subtle light! How was this possible? Her eyes darted to the bowl of warm water in which Lotus Blossom had soaked Trixie's hoof. Suddenly, the moment came rushing back to her. She'd been onstage in a curtain of mist when her hoof had become magical in the first place . . .

"Ha!" Trixie shouted in triumph as she sprang to her wet hooves. It was *water*. Her eyes looked wild. "My magical hoof is back and I know how to keep it! There's no stopping me from getting into the Starmane Society of Magicians now!" Trixie tore the towel from her pale-blue mane and tossed it aside. Then she cast a cloud of smoke and disappeared to Luna knew where.

"Rarity!" Starlight Glimmer burst into the room. She was out of breath, having galloped all the way from the Everfree Forest. "Have you seen Trixie?! We have to stop her before she ruins all of Ponyville by accident!"

Rarity put her hoof to her head and sighed. "Can't a mare have one little, teensy spa hour without some epic drama?"

Starlight looked at her frantically. "Guess not?"

"Fair enough, darling." Rarity stood up, tossed some bits to Aloe and Lotus Blossom, and nodded at Starlight. "Now let's go help that crazy pony!"

Chapter

8

Follow the Yellow Trick Road

✶ ✶ ✶

The castle wasn't far from the center of
Ponyville, but Trixie had forgotten just how
heavy her hoof was while under the spell.
Every step took twice as long as she trudged
through the winding backstreets, dragging
her hoof over the cobblestones. She shot

a burst of magic at it, hoping to employ a featherlight spell to ease the weight. The zap took no effect, pinging on the glowing surface with a tiny fizz.

"This is oh-so tedious and tiresome!" Trixie groaned. It was taking forever to get back to her wagon! She was so eager to arrive because once she was there, Trixie planned to revamp her whole act to feature her brand-new special talent.

There would be water, there would be light, and there would be tons of sparkling gems. It would take some extra work to figure out, but it would be well worth it. Trixie was positive that she would be standing next to Starmane herself, exchanging secret illusionist tips and magician gossip over ciders in no time.

"Trixie!" Starlight Glimmer called out from behind her, yanking Trixie from her lofty daydreams. "Wait up!"

The blue Unicorn spun around to see Starlight and Rarity galloping toward her. Unsurprisingly, they had concerned expressions on their faces.

Everypony in Ponyville was always either grinning like a filly in a candy shop or fretting about a "friendship problem." *Here we go again*, thought Trixie. She steeled herself for a lecture.

"Sorry I had to duck out of the spa like that," Trixie apologized. She was careful to hide her golden hoof inside her starry cloak. "I had a great idea for my show and had to leave immediately before I forgot what it was." She smiled nervously at Rarity. "You know how it is when inspiration strikes! Got to grab it by the hoof...."

"Of course," Rarity replied with a nod and a smile. "The magic muse is a fickle mare!" Her eyes darted to Starlight Glimmer. She made a dainty grunting noise. Either she was developing a nasty cold or it was some sort of code between the two of them. Trixie raised a suspicious eyebrow.

"We wanted to talk to you about something," Starlight offered brightly. "It won't take long...."

Suddenly, a cloud of smoke burst among the ponies! Starlight and Rarity coughed and sputtered, looking around for Trixie. A moment later when it cleared, they expected Trixie to have vanished as per usual, but she was only a few steps farther away. Trixie stomped her normal hoof on the ground in frustration. Her usual tricks were no good with her heavy hoof. "*Awww.* That was my last smoke bomb, too."

She turned back to her friends. "Whatever it is, it'll have to wait," Trixie replied in a huff. "If I'm going to be ready with a whole new act in time for the Starmane Society ball, I need to get to work designing my new incredible, astonishing, flabbergasting feat of . . ." She trailed off, distracted by a small group of ponies gathering in the distance. They seemed to be inspecting something on the ground. Perhaps a pony had lost her coin purse.

"More Glowpaz!" yelled Scootaloo. The filly kicked her hoof on the piece, but it was lodged in the ground.

"I don't believe it. It's everywhere!" said Filthy Rich, leaning down. His eyes began to twinkle with greedy anticipation. He looked around at the crowd, realizing his mistake. "I mean...uh... *never mind*! Nothing to see here! Go away!" The stallion plopped down his flank, trying to hide the gem until he could extract it and keep it for himself.

The group began to grow larger as more curious ponies stopped to check out the source of the commotion. Trixie couldn't help herself. She had to see it for herself! She galloped to the group, Rarity and Starlight following close behind.

It didn't take long for everypony to see that the brightest glow of all was standing right among them—it was Trixie herself. She shifted back and forth on her hooves, making a little pattern on the ground. The stones beneath her lit up with each step and began to pulse with the trademark glow of the rare gem.

"Look..." said a pale-yellow Pegasus. "Everything Trixie touches...turns to Glowpaz!"

"*Whoaaaa.*" The townsponies cooed in awe. Rarity and Starlight exchanged a nervous look. It looked like Twilight *was* right, and the magic was starting to affect Trixie more and more.

It was *true*. Even the direct path in which Trixie had trotted from the spa was now littered with a glittering trail of remnants. For whatever strange reason, Trixie's hoof had progressed from just creating Glowpaz out of water droplets. It had been cursed with the ability to turn *anything*, even ordinary stones, into rare jewels.

"Stand back! The Brilliant and Luminous Trixie has important things to do!" she barked. "But if you'd like to see more of this magnificent marvel, come to my show in Canterlot! Tomorrow."

Trixie was bursting at the thought of using her newfound power to impress the Starmane Society.

Visions of being greeted with open hooves in far-off cities and exotic lands taunted her. In them, Trixie would be more than just a Society magician—she would be the successor to Starmane's legacy herself: a glowing goddess with the ability to entertain and delight by spectacularly creating beautiful, sparkling gems. Ponies would fall at her hooves in reverence for her magical expertise and unique gift.

Tomorrow was Trixie's night. She felt a sense of duty to give her admirers what they were clamoring for and to show those Star-mane Society ponies she was the cream of the crop right away! All Trixie needed was a little water to make it rain.

Chapter

9

Grim Prospects

★ ★ ★

Back at the castle, Twilight was in a tizzy. She'd asked for Applejack, Fluttershy, Pinkie Pie, and Rainbow Dash to join her in the throne room. The five ponies sat facing one another, as they usually did when there was some sort of crisis.

"But why are all those ponies camping here?" Rainbow Dash puzzled. "We've never had them visit Ponyville before, right?"

"Prospectors go where the wind whispers to 'em," Applejack explained with a shrug. "They hear about a pony strikin' it rich this way or that, and they'll be there, staking a claim on it."

Twilight shook her head. "Have you seen what they've done to Ponyville Park?" She flung up her hooves. "Holes dug everywhere!"

"You bet I have!" Fluttershy fumed. Her voice was just slightly louder than its normal volume of a sweet, gentle whisper. "The poor little animals are terrified. Just terrified." Fluttershy looked like she was going to cry. "Their homes just dug into and ripped apart…"

"So what should we do?" Rainbow Dash looked around to each of their faces. "Ask them to leave?" The blue Pegasus fidgeted with her rainbow mane.

"You can give it a whirl, but chances are they won't budge," Applejack cautioned. She looked to Rainbow Dash. "There was a gold rush once in Appleloosa. Took ponies moons to leave, even once the stream dried up."

"I hope Starlight Glimmer was able to find Trixie," Twilight Sparkle fretted. "If she is cursed with a Gem Hoof like we fear, we don't have much time until she's in danger.... It takes a little bit, but the Gem Hoof eventually affects the cursed pony's entire body. If we're too late, Trixie could be completely transformed into a gem statue!" Twilight bit her lip and stared up at the chandelier, pushing the horrible thought from her mind. "I just wish I knew who cursed her and why!"

"*Oooh! Oooh!*" Pinkie Pie squealed as she squirmed in her throne, hoof raised. "I think I know!"

Applejack frowned. "Well, why didn't ya say so, sugarcube?"

"Yeah. What happened?!" Rainbow Dash urged.

"Well…" Pinkie took a deep breath and spoke very quickly. "Trixie was bugging Rarity to make her an outfit, but then she tried to mess with the dress Rarity was sewing for Sapphire Shores and got in the way, and Rarity's magic went all loopsy-doodles! So then Trixie's hoof was like, '*gloooow!*' and everypony in town was like, '*whoaaaaa!*' and now everything she touches is totally turning into Glowpaz!" Pinkie shrugged. "I saw it happen through the window."

The ponies were all taken aback, but the color drained from Twilight's face. "It was *Rarity*? And it was an accident?" Now *that* she didn't expect. But Twilight did know magic's effect worked with intent. Rarity's magic was intended for the dress—not Trixie. So would the remedy need to change, too? Between Twilight's and Starlight's skills, they stood a good chance of figuring it out. But they didn't have much time.

"We have to find Trixie right away and reverse that spell—before it's too late!"

If they didn't, Trixie would soon become nothing more than a great and powerful statue—forever frozen in Glowpaz like a fly in a piece of amber.

Chapter

10

The Radiance Remedy

★ ★ ★

Oh no! The spot in the field where Trixie's wagon had been parked for the past few days was now decidedly empty. All that remained were a few wayward playing cards and a glowing trail of Glowpaz dust.

"She's gone!" Pinkie Pie squealed in genuine shock. The pink pony began to poke around the bushes as if she were playing a game of hide-and-seek. "Like, *gone* gone!"

"Where do you think she could've gone?" Rainbow Dash wondered aloud as Applejack kicked the dirt with her hoof and leaned down to inspect a piece of Glowpaz.

"She couldn't have gotten too far." Twilight looked off into the distance. "If the curse has taken effect enough for her to be leaving a trail, then her hoof should be getting pretty heavy by now." In fact, the more Trixie used her magic, the faster the curse would take full effect. Twilight hoped that the Unicorn was being judicious with her spells.

Starlight and Rarity came galloping across the field. They looked like they'd seen a ghost on Nightmare Night. "There you are!" Starlight exclaimed to her group of friends. "Rarity and I have been looking all over for you."

"Do you know where Trixie is?" asked Twilight, feeling anxious. They may not have always gotten along, but the last thing Twilight wanted was for anything to happen to her. "We need to find her right away!"

Rarity's eyes darted around nervously. "She's gone to Canterlot to put on a show. There was no stopping her. Also, I think I may have possibly accidentally, erm…oh dear, how should I put this? Well…I didn't mean to but…I *cursed her*!"

As the Friendship Express chugged through the countryside to the capital city, Rarity clutched her dress bag protectively. Every-pony deserved to look their best, and even if the garment wasn't perfect, it would still help to convince Trixie that Rarity cared about her. She really hadn't meant any harm.

"Isn't it fascinating how magic can be so fickle and tricky?" Rarity laughed nervously. "One minute, a pony can be sending swirls of pretty light at her celebrity Glammys gown, and the next she could be accidentally zapping a pony's hoof and causing an obscure curse to take effect!"

"Don't feel bad, Rarity," Twilight said, shooting her pal a sympathetic look. "It was an accident."

"The important part is that we were able to find some of the Gleam Berries in the castle stores," Starlight reminded everypony. "The Radiance Remedy potion Twilight whipped up should work to restore Trixie."

"That is, if she'll drink it!" Rainbow Dash scoffed. "Good luck prying a special power out of that pony's hooves. Remember the Alicorn Amulet?"

The ponies all exchanged an awkward look. They knew that Trixie had apologized for the incident in which she'd exiled Twilight from Ponyville out of jealousy for her magic skills. And she had definitely changed for the better. But still, there was a sliver of doubt in each of their minds....

Starlight Glimmer, however, knew a different side of Trixie. She'd come through for her on a number of occasions. Starlight owed her best friend. "One way or another, I will find a way to get this tonic into her and cure Trixie." Starlight held up the bottle to the light for a closer inspection. There was barely a sip's worth inside.

"Better get it right on the first try," Applejack warned with a furrowed brow. "That amount there couldn't quench a flea's thirst."

One drop would do the trick.

Chapter

11

Cloak and Swagger

★ ★ ★

Word had spread quickly about the magnificent mare with the Glowpaz hoof. Ponies across the kingdom had the name *Trixie* on their lips. Everypony wanted to see her in action and catch a piece of the glowing bounty.

Once she'd arrived in Canterlot, Trixie had taken her time setting up the stage.

Partly because she wanted to build suspense, and partly because she was physically unable to move very fast with her heavy hoof. Why did it feel like her entire foreleg was heavier now, too?

Trixie was just finishing the task of unfurling her new giant "The Hoof That Holds the Glowpaz" posters when she heard the annoying babble of a loud group of friends yelling some nonsense at her. Trixie covered her left ear and winced in mock pain. "Trixie's ears are delicate! Why must you make such terrible sounds at me?"

"Don't go onstage!" Twilight shouted.

"Stop the show!" cried Fluttershy.

"Pretty please?" Rarity whined.

Trixie looked at them and laughed. "I'm going to razzle-dazzle every single pony out there because it's the only chance I have to impress the ponies of the Starmane Society of Magicians. They are *right* across the street as we speak!" She rolled her eyes. "You came all the way to Canterlot to try to stop all that? That's not very friendly! Aren't you all supposed to be the experts in that department?" She looked right at Twilight for the last part.

The sky was beginning to darken. Trixie's hoof and foreleg were beginning to look even more brilliant in the low light. Rarity couldn't tear her eyes away from the way the light was creeping onto Trixie's back.

"*Listen* to me!" Starlight begged. Her purple-and-teal mane swayed in the breeze as she pointed to Trixie's bright shoulder. "You have to stop your hoof from glowing or else it's going to spread. It will turn you into a very...pretty...glowing...*statue*!"

"I don't believe you," Trixie replied with a sassy expression. She began to trot away. "This is all just a ploy to take the attention away from me again, isn't it?"

"No, of course not," Twilight Sparkle replied sincerely. "We're your friends!"

Trixie scoffed. "My show is starting in three minutes, and I hope you will all be in the audience to support me." She stuck her nose in the air and turned back to look at them. "You know, what *friends* do."

The magician trotted off backstage to prepare. Starlight followed her. "I'm going to fix this," she told the others. "I promise."

Starlight remained hidden as Trixie puttered around, checking props and peeking around the curtain to look at the growing crowd outside. There were hundreds of ponies waiting to catch a glimpse of the famous glowing hoof! When Trixie went to adjust the faucet on the hose, a light-bulb went off in Starlight's head. That was it! Starlight could administer the Radiance Remedy through a random water mist, just like she'd done at the other show. Then Trixie would be doused in the magical tonic and be saved.

Starlight felt better instantly. All she had to do now was wait for the right cue.

Chapter

12

Torn and Restored

★ ★ ★

"Welcome to the most marvelous sight you will ever see! Mares and gentlecolts, I present to you...without further ado...the *one*...the only...the always-glowing, gem-giving, incredible illusionist...THE GREAT AND POWERFUL *TRIXIEEEE*!" Trixie burst onto the stage in a flash of light.

The crowd gasped at the shocking sight of her. Half of Trixie's body was glowing! Trixie looked down at herself and her eyes went large. She quickly covered up her surprise and continued on, limping across the stage in an awkward fashion. "The Great and Powerful Trixie will now perform a never-before-attempted, one-of-a-kind stunning stunt—'The Hoof That Holds the Glowpaz!"

Trixie held up her shining hoof. The brilliant light illuminated the crazed expression on her face. "Behold...my hoof of wonder!" She waved her hoof in the air and began pacing the stage slowly. Her body felt quite heavy. Everypony in the crowd followed her with their eyes, back and forth. "I will now transform any item, of any substance, into a beautiful jewel!"

"Any item at all!" Suddenly, Starlight Glimmer appeared, wearing a sequined bow tie and skirt. She struck a pose and flashed a cheesy smile. Then she stepped forward and did a dramatic twirl. Starlight pranced over to a young colt in the front row and leaned down.

"Do you have an item you'd like the Great and Powerful Trixie to transform, young sir?" The colt reluctantly passed her his stuffed toy bear.

Trixie shot an angry look at Starlight. Who did she think she was, trying to ruin the show?

"When do we get the Glowpaz rain?" a random mare shouted from the audience. "Hurry up!"

Trixie ignored her and continued on. "Behold…behold…"

"Behold the beautiful glowing hoof as this bear becomes made of precious gems!" Starlight finished with a wink. "And that's not all, folks—by the end of this show, so will Trixie herself become fully made of Glowpaz!" The audience gasped and erupted into applause. Even Trixie looked surprised.

"That's right!" Trixie hollered. "I will transform and return to normal, unscathed by the unbearable weight and considerable— *Ahhhh, oohh!*" Trixie fell over on her side, like a wooden pony doll. Her legs stuck straight out, immobilized in their glowing casts.

The audience started laughing. Trixie's face burned with embarrassment. She tried to get up but just scooted across the stage.

Twilight, Fluttershy, Rainbow Dash, Pinkie Pie, Rarity, and Applejack watched in agony from the audience. Fluttershy covered her eyes and whimpered helplessly.

Even though it was earlier than she'd anticipated, Starlight Glimmer couldn't wait another second. She wheeled out the hose from backstage, cranked it on, and poured the Radiance Remedy right into the misty stream, blasting it all the way over to Trixie!

As soon as the potion hit Trixie's hide, a blinding light surged through the entire street and a ringing sound pierced everypony's ears.

The ponies blinked away the stars in their eyes that had been left by the light of the spell taking effect. The audience stumbled around, grasping for their hoofing, and began wandering off in a confused stupor. The show was over.

Starlight Glimmer rubbed at her eyes. When her sight finally returned, she saw Trixie curled into a tiny ball on the ground. Her eyes were closed tight. "Is it over?" she whimpered. "Is my beautiful, magical glow hoof *gone*?"

"I'm afraid so." Starlight reached out and helped Trixie up again. She felt as light as a feather. "But thank Celestia!" Starlight broke into a genuine smile. "I was so worried about you. And I really wasn't sure if changing the show like that would work!"

"So…" Trixie sighed and smiled back. "I guess you were right about the whole glowing-statue thing." She plopped down on the ground and shook her head. "I'm sorry I got so carried away again. I just really wanted to impress the ponies from the Starmane Society so badly!"

"We know, sugarcube." Applejack smiled reassuringly at her. "Maybe there'll be another chance?"

"I thought...that if they saw my glow hoof, they might think I was special...." Trixie explained.

"You are special. And the thing we love about you most, Trixie, is that you never give up!" Twilight admitted with a grin. The others nodded in encouraging agreement. They were all impressed by how quickly Trixie had bounced back. "That's a quality that everypony admires."

"I didn't get to give this to you earlier," Rarity said, stepping forward. She unzipped the dress bag, revealing a perfectly stitched, one-of-a-kind cloak. Trixie's jaw dropped. "I wanted to say sorry for... uh...the whole hoof thing." Rarity laughed nervously.

"Whoa!" Trixie swung the new cloak around her body. It was smooth, shimmery, and showy—perfect in every way. "Thank you so much." Trixie was so touched, she looked like she might cry. "I don't deserve friends like all of you."

"Of course you do!" they replied in unison. Everypony enveloped Trixie in a traditional group hug.

"I'm still going to find a way to impress the Society, if I can." Trixie grinned, the wheels turning in her head already. "Maybe I can try to come up with a whole new never-before-attempted feat...something involving crocodiles—"

"Excuse me?" an older mare dripping with emeralds interrupted, stepping forward. "The Great and Powerful Trixie, I presume?" Her silver mane was laden with shimmering stars and she wore a mischievous expression on her face. "I'm—"

"Starmane!" Trixie gasped in reverence. "Wow. Of course I know who you are."

"That was quite the amusing performance you put on," she said with a sly smile. "Such a clever show. I loved how you pretended to not know what the act was! I haven't laughed that much since I saw 'The Hilarious and Amazing Piebald'!"

"Oh, thank you..." Trixie replied, feeling an odd mixture of starstruck and confused. She looked to her friends. They were all grinning and motioning excitedly.

Starmane cocked her head to the side. "Say, Trixie...would you like to come join me and the others for a mug of cider across the street? Tonight's our big Society ball, and we could certainly use some new blood to liven up the party!"

"Trixie would love nothing more!"

Chapter

13

The Starmane Society Ball

★ ★ ★

Trixie stood before the enigmatic members of the Starmane Society of Magicians. Candles floated everywhere, and there was soft, jazzy music playing throughout the secret lounge below the ballroom.

It was a more-than-suitable setting for an exclusive Society party, Trixie thought as she spun around dramatically. Her brand-new shiny cloak of swirling colors swung out and landed softly upon her pale-blue shoulders. A devious look sparkled in her violet eyes. "And that, Society members, is the tale of how my friends and I saved Equestria from the most fearsome villains known to ponykind—the evil Queen Chrysalis and her army of love-sucking changelings!"

"Well done!" commended a magician named The Daring and Fearless Wild Card. He tipped his shimmering black top hat to her. A white dove flew out and perched upon another magician's head.

"Cheers to you!" said a Pegasus aptly named The Incredible and Gifted Gimmick as she passed Trixie a glass of cider. "You had me on the edge of my seat. True entertainment!"

Trixie nodded in agreement, a slight blush on her face. Starmane herself had been listening to the story. The old mare gave a nod of approval and slowly made her way over to Trixie. Her jewels *clink-clank*ed together and her long, royal-blue velvet cloak floated along the floor. It felt like Trixie's heart was going to beat right out of her chest.

"You may be a bit different, but you're spunky, young filly! You're a true enter-tainer. That's something we here admire very much and need more of in our esteemed group." Starmane put a hoof on Trixie's shoulder. "So, I believe this belongs to you, O Great and Powerful Trixie..." There, in Starmane's very hoof, was the only thing that Trixie had dreamed about, the only thing that meant more than glowing

riches or endless praise from audiences—
a Starmane Society of Magicians official
member brooch!

"I...I..." Trixie sputtered as she stud-
ied the symbol of the two crossed wands
surrounded by a halo of stars. "I'm in awe.
Thank you, Stupendous and Astounding
Starmane!"

The ponies erupted into convivial laugh-
ter and applause. Trixie took a deep bow,
trying to keep a serious magician's face. But
she couldn't help but grin. She was really
here; she was really a part of this! Every
ounce of Trixie felt truly magical, right
down to the tips of her hooves.

Turn the page for
a special surprise from
Trixie!

Dear Reader,

I hope you enjoy these very special bonus pages! I took time out of my busy and incredibly interesting schedule to put them together just for you. Have fun filling them out and sharing them with all your friends!

Yours in Excellence,

The Great and Powerful Trixie

A Very Special Cloak

The Great and Powerful Trixie is feeling the need for a new cloak to perfect her next big show. Draw the most special, magical, and glorious cloak you can for her!

Golden Apples

Trixie accidentally turned some of Applejack's crop into precious stones! Can you find the 5 transformed gems in the image below?

BEST FRIENDS FOREVER!

The Great and Powerful Trixie doesn't have all that many friends—she's just so great and powerful, other ponies are intimidated by her brilliance. But her very best friend in the world, Starlight Glimmer, loves spending time and playing games with her. Grab a friend and play some Dots or Tic-Tac-Toe!

FIND THE MAGIC WORDS!

Magic can be a tricky thing. And some magicians, although (almost) never the Great and Powerful Trixie, have a hard time getting their spells just perfect. Help find the special words below so novice ponies can work their magic! Words can be found foreward, backward, upside down, and diagonally.

```
N A C W T J E S R U
F O A L A F N N U Y
K N I U O R D O N T
D I F S O A O I E P
Q X B C U V K T S D
W V I U R L G O R D
A N K D M D L P V T
U R A B B I T I F T
K O O B L L E P S X
U L E L E P D R O S
```

CLOAK   **ILLUSION** **POTIONS**
RABBIT   **RUNES**   **SPELLBOOK**
UNICORN   **WAND**

The Starmane Society of Magicians

Equestria has its fair share of super-famous magicians, including, obviously, the Great and Powerful Trixie. Use the space below to draw the most powerful pony wizard you can imagine!

MAGICAL POWERS FOR ALL!

Sure, Trixie has all the magical powers
she could ever want. But what would _you_ do if
you had the ability to cast awesome spells? Write
what you would do if you had one day with the
ability to do magic!

_____

_____

_____

_____

_____

_____

_____

_____

_____

THE SAME-STAGE SITUATION

Trixie loves putting on magic shows wherever she goes, and she always does a little better if the stages she performs on are exactly the same. There are 7 differences between the two stages below. Can you find them all?

THE QUICKEST WAY TO THE LIBRARY

It's a Ponyville emergency! Trixie seems to have been cursed with a Midas hoof, and her only hope for help is if Princess Twilight Sparkle can reach her books in time! Help her take the quickest route there!

START

FINISH

FRIENDSHIP LESSON #189

Trixie is still waiting for all the ponies of Equestria to trust her fully after her slightly-villainous-but-<u>really</u>-just-misunderstood past. Twilight and the rest of her friends have been able to forgive her, though. Write about a time when one of your friends messed up and needed forgiveness.

_____

_____

_____

_____

_____

_____

_____

_____

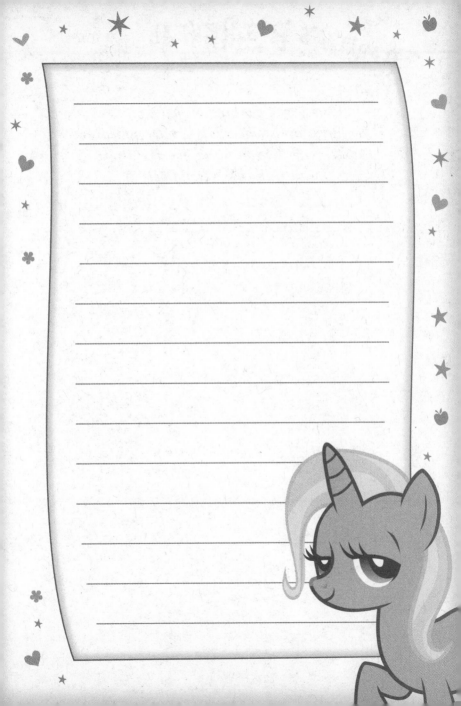

Rarity's Big Reveal

Rarity was working on her next
beautiful dress when Trixie interrupted
her. Draw what you think her next, next
beautiful dress should be!